D0337160

This Little Tiger
book belongs to:

_____

_____

05222778

LITTLE TIGER PRESS LTD
an imprint of the Little Tiger Group
1 The Coda Centre,
189 Munster Road,
London SW6 6AW
www.littletiger.co.uk

First published in Great Britain 2014
Text by Mara Alperin
Text copyright © Little Tiger Press 2014
Illustrations copyright © Nick East 2014
Nick East has asserted his right to be identified as
the illustrator of this work under the Copyright,
Designs and Patents Act, 1988
A CIP catalogue record for this book is
available from the British Library
All rights reserved

ISBN 978-1-84895-710-7
Printed in China
LTP/1900/1773/1216
4 6 8 10 9 7 5 3

To Emily, Meagan, Mary and Tom ~ MA

With love to Janet and Doug x ~ NE

Chicken Licken

Mara Alperin

Illustrated by Nick East

LITTLE TIGER PRESS
London

On a sunny farm there lived a fuzzy, yellow chick called Chicken Licken. He was happy and hoppy... but he wasn't the brightest chicken in the coop.

Radish

Cabbage

Carrots

Lettuce

One warm autumn day, Chicken Licken
was hop-skip-skipping through the woods,
when suddenly an acorn dropped
from a tree, and bounced
off his head . . .

Click!

Clack!

Clonk!

"Oh, my feathers! Was that a piece of sky?" he squeaked. "Help! Oh, help!"

hen house

Trembling, Chicken Licken scurried back to the hen house, squawking, "The sky is falling! The sky is falling!"

Henny
Penny

"What's **all** this
noise?" clucked
Henny Penny.

"The sky is falling!"
panted Chicken Licken.
"It went Click! Clack!
Clonk!
right on my
head!"

Henny Penny dropped
her spectacles. "Dear me!"
she gasped. "We must tell
the King. He'll know
what to do!"

So Chicken Licken and
Henny Penny ran over
to the duck pond,
squawking and clucking,
"The sky is falling!
We must find the King!"

"Did I hear the sky is falling?" quacked Ducky Lucky.

"Yes, it fell on my head – Click! Clack! Clonk!" said Chicken Licken.

"What will we do?" cried Ducky Lucky. "The King will save us," Henny Penny clucked. "We must find him at once!"

So Chicken Licken,
Henny Penny and
Ducky Lucky dashed off again,
squawking and clucking
and quacking,
"The sky
is falling!
We must find
the King!"

"The sky is falling?" gobbled Turkey Lurkey. "Quick! Take cover!" And he **leaped** into the bushes to hide.

"The sky is falling?"

"There's **no** time to lose!" cried Chicken Licken. "We **must** hurry to town to find **the King!**"

So Chicken Licken, Henny Penny, Ducky Lucky and Turkey Lurkey charged down the path, shouting . . .

"The **sky** is **falling!** We **must** find the King! But it wasn't the King they saw . . .

. . . It was Foxy Loxy.

"What seems to be the matter, my fine feathered friends?" grinned Foxy Loxy.

"The sky is falling!" puffed Chicken Licken. "We must tell the King!"

Foxy Loxy licked his lips.
  "Poor little birds," he smirked.
"Come with me, and *I'll* help
      you find the King!"

And so Foxy Loxy led the search for the King. The animals started in the bookshop . . .

"The King's not in here," said Foxy Loxy, peeping into a recipe book.

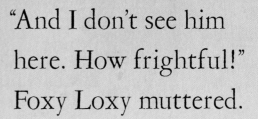

Can you see him?

"And I don't see him here. How frightful!" Foxy Loxy muttered.

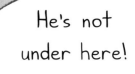

He's not under here!

Spice up your dinner!

Spicier

Hot!!

"Now I remember where the King is!" Foxy Loxy said with a sly smile. "I invited him to my den for dinner. Oh, do say you'll join our **feast**…"

"Don't worry, my tasty little friends – it's not much further to my den," chuckled Foxy Loxy, starting to drool …

Foxy Loxy opened the door, and the birds waddled slowly inside.

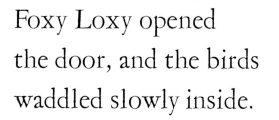

It was cold and dark in Foxy Loxy's den. "I don't see the King," muttered Henny Penny. "Perhaps he's running late."

"I can't see anything at all!" whispered Chicken Licken.

Then Foxy Loxy
lit the chandelier. "It's almost
time for dinner," he purred.
"What's for dinner?" asked
Ducky Lucky.

"You are!" cried Foxy Loxy.
And he leaped
at the birds . . .

"Help!"

they all cried.

"Help!"

And they squawked and screeched and fluttered and flapped until the whole den shook and the chandelier fell – Click! Clack! Clonk! onto Foxy Loxy's head!

"Yikes!" shrieked Foxy Loxy. "The **sky really is falling!**"

And he dashed away as fast as he could, straight into . . .

...the King!

"Greetings!" crowed the King. "What's this
I hear about the sky falling? The whole town
is in a flutter! But look, dear friends –
the great, blue sky is still up there."

Chicken Licken gazed up, and he saw that the King was right. So the birds hop-skip-skipped under the bright sky all afternoon. And they never saw Foxy Loxy **ever** again!

My First Fairy Tales

are familiar, fun and friendly
stories – with a marvellously
modern twist!

The Three Little Pigs

Jack and the Beanstalk

Rumpelstiltskin

The Gingerbread Man

The Ugly Duckling

The Elves and the Shoemaker

Chicken Licken

The Three Billy Goats Gruff

Little Red Riding Hood

Goldilocks and the Three Bears